INTERSECTION ALLIES

We Make Room for All

By Chelsea Johnson, LaToya Council, and Carolyn Choi

Illustrations by Ashley Seil Smith

dottir press

NEW YORK CITY

Published in 2019 by Dottir Press
33 Fifth Avenue
New York, NY 10003

Dottirpress.com

Third printing June 2020
Illustrations by Ashley Seil Smith
Production by Drew Stevens

Trade distribution by Consortium Book Sales and Distribution,
www.cbsd.com. For inquiries about bulk sales, please contact
jb@dottirpress.com.

Library of Congress Cataloging-in-Publication Data is available for this title.
ISBN 978-1-948340-08-3

PRINTED IN THE UNITED STATES OF AMERICA BY WORZALLA

To each other—we're better together.

FOREWORD

When we think of childhood and early education, we tend to remember learning things like numbers and letters, colors and shapes, timetables and table manners. What's less often considered is that youth is also an opportunity for planting the seeds of social conscience. The impressions of the world that we gather as children become the foundations for how we understand our places in it as adults. What might the future look like if all children were taught about justice, equity, and solidarity alongside the alphabet and arithmetic?

IntersectionAllies: We Make Room for All is an invaluable tool for bringing about such a future. This entertaining and informative book teaches young readers that despite all of the ways we are different from one another, we still have values and common interests that intersect. We can listen to and support each other in ways that unite us across differences.

Thirty years ago, I coined intersectionality as a framework for a social justice agenda that includes all oppressed people. It's humbling and energizing to see the many ways intersectionality continues to inspire and empower social justice advocates today. I'm delighted that *IntersectionAllies: We Make Room for All* will pass the torch to the next generation of youth activists. Like the powerful young people in this book, I believe we are strongest when we build communities that are founded on the understanding that we have a stake in each other.

—Dr. Kimberlé Crenshaw, African American Policy Forum
Co-Founder and Director of the Columbia Law School Center
for Intersectionality and Social Policy Studies

A Letter To Grown-Ups

Dear Grown-ups:

It is a classic parenting dilemma: How do we teach children how to treat each other in a world that promotes all the wrong lessons? How do we teach lessons that don't repeat the mistakes we have made ourselves?

IntersectionAllies: We Make Room for All answers these questions with empathy and clarity. This book provides an introduction to the concepts of allyship and intersectionality for elementary school-aged children and their families, using the simple idea of "making room." "Making room" goes beyond allowing somebody physical space. It means acknowledging our complex identities as sources of power within classrooms, communities, and cultures rather than treating difference as a threat, vulnerability, or a source of shame.

"Making room" is stronger than ideas like "respect" and "tolerance" because it asks for a positive action from us rather than a minimal response. In order for us to gain an ally, we must be an ally, and do so in a way that combines initiative, solidarity, cooperation, and trustworthiness. In other words, don't wait for someone else to do it! In this book, allies help Gloria and Heejung recognize the value of their translation capabilities rather than feel shame about their families.

Allie, Kate, and Nia show us that we need to make room over and over again. "Making room" is a habit of solidarity, like getting up every morning and brushing your teeth. It is something that is necessary to do over and over again to be healthy. When you first learn solidarity you may make mistakes. But like brushing your teeth, you get better at it with practice. You will notice when you skipped over a tooth or ate too much candy, and how to adjust your actions in the future for better results. Solidarity is something anyone can learn and everyone needs to learn.

The children portrayed in this book have diverse identities, the combinations of which set each of them apart. Intersectionality recognizes that we cannot divide ourselves into parts. We can't be only our gender on Mondays and Wednesdays or only our race on Tuesdays and Thursdays. *IntersectionAllies* reminds us that we don't have to "choose" one primary identity. Instead, each of us is all of who we are every single day and in every single way.

This book also shows that some kids face challenges that are not simply personal—the issues they face often involve challenges from social, political, and economic powers. Drawing upon children's need for safety, Dakota, Yuri, and Nia each illustrate how governments are also places where room needs to be made. The authors, three young sociologists, demonstrate that while we are all a combination of identities, we are also people navigating social structures and institutions that aren't always set up to "make room" for us.

In choosing to introduce solidarity and intersectionality to children, the authors have opened up ideas about how we all might "make room" for people and groups who are not like us.

—Dr. Ange-Marie Hancock Alfaro,
Chair, Gender and Sexuality Studies Department,
University of Southern California

Witness the lives of a bold group of friends.
If one is in need, another defends.
Age is one trait that each of them share,
But kids' lives are unique, as you'll soon be aware.
Each child has a story and their own point of view
Filled with passion and power, just like you.

My name is Alejandra, but I go by Allie.
I use a chair, but it doesn't define me.
Instead, it allows me to

ZZZZIP
GLIDE
and
PLAY.

When I need to get through, friends help make a way.

where there's room FOR SOME

we make room FOR ALL

friends can be ALLIES no matter how small!

Hello, I'm Parker! After school every day,
Allie's family takes care of us both while we play.

My mom works hard to provide for me.
Her love's the source of our stability.

Not toys or money, nor treasures untold—
Community care is more precious than gold.

Skirts and frills are cute, I suppose,
But my superhero cape is more "Kate" than those bows.

Some may be confused that a kid like me
Can wear what I want and be proud and carefree.
My friends defend my choices and place.
A bathroom, like all rooms, should be a safe space.

19

My name is Adilah, and just like Kate,
What I wear inspires endless debate.
Some give, some chant, some sing, some pray,
My hijab is my choice—you can choose your own way.

The clothes that you wear never justify hatred.
Clothes can be playful, simple, or sacred.
Covered, adorned, or with casual flair,
My body's my own, I dress it with care!

My name is Nia, and with what's on the news
It's easy to be frightened or sing the blues.

For her, for them, for him, and for me
We all deserve to breathe and be free.

The color of our skin is no reason to hide.
We protest for safety, equality, and pride.

Our friends join along in solidarity and love.
This is the stuff that allies are made of!

SAY HER NAME

INTERSECTIONALITY IS FOR EVERYBODY

BLACK LIVES MATTER

ALLY

Safety also includes our trees and air,
The land we've called home, our places of prayer.
I am Dakota, and like my ancestors,
My tribe and I are water protectors.
From profit and power, we stand up to preserve
Our nations, our cultures, and the respect we deserve.

My name is Gloria, *y tengo siete años.*
After school, it's to *la frutería* I go.
Trabajo cada día junto a mi madre.
Vendemos piña dulce y mangos con chile.

My language and savvy allow us to thrive.
I've got hopes and dreams and skills and drive!
Working together makes us both more secure.
I'm a daughter, a partner, and an entrepreneur.

My name is Heejung, and I was born in Seoul.
I moved here when I was five years old.
I'm part of what's called the "1.5 generation."
My parents and I span two different nations.

슈퍼

Like Gloria, I am a help to my mother
By translating for her one word to another.
When the landlord tells mom, "You can pay me next Friday,"
I repeat in Korean: "*Omma renteu daeum ju geumyoire naedo doendae!*"
We navigate life in our new home together,
'Cause kids have the skills to make every day better!

OFFICE

33

My name is Yuri and I'm new to this place.
Heejung's family welcomed me with love and with grace.
Finding refuge meant traveling far from home.
I sailed, I flew, I rode, and I roamed.
Escaping violence, war, heartache, and intrusion,
We came to this nation seeking dreams and inclusion.

From near, from far, from here, from there—

We're more than our origins. We all deserve care.

Race, religion, citizenship, class, and ability:
Each of these intersects to form identity.
Age, gender, size, and skin color, too,
Can make living life different for a friend than for you.

Barriers and biases are often to blame.
We strive to be equal but not all the same.

Life's ups and downs can take many forms,
But standing together, we'll rewrite the norms.

where there's room
FOR SOME
we make room
FOR ALL

friends can be ALLIES no matter how small!

What Is Intersectionality?

Intersectionality is a word that explains how all of the different parts of a person combine to affect their life experiences and personal identity. Age, ability, skin color, religion, citizenship, body size, and culture all make up our personal identity and influence who we are and how we live.

There are things about each character in this book that shape their feelings and experiences. For example, Nia's worries about the criminal justice system (our courts, police, and jails) are shaped by her gender and race, while Adilah's clothing choices are shaped by her gender, culture, and religion. **Take a moment to think about your own experiences and identity. What are some things that make you, you?**

The idea of intersectionality not only helps us understand who we are; it can also help us think about how we relate to other people. Thinking about race, class, gender, citizenship, and other identities together (rather than separately) can help us notice more opportunities for solidarity with people who are different from us.

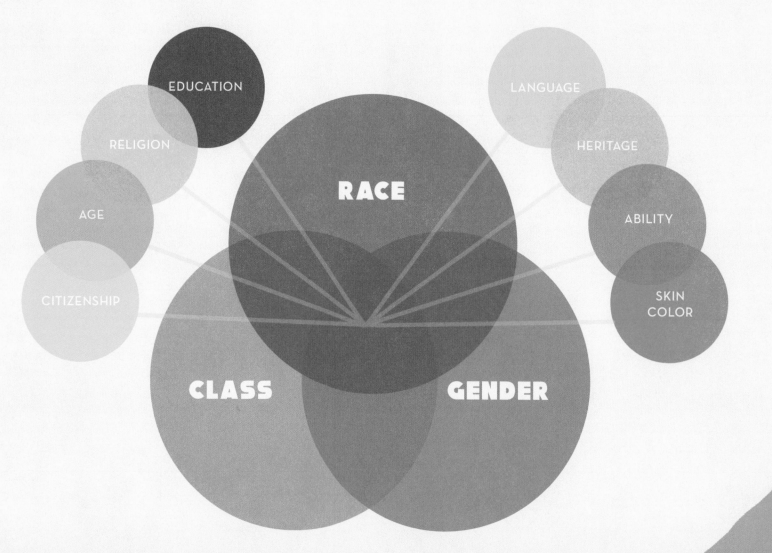

For instance, even though the legal system in the United States has often discriminated against African American women like Nia and her mother, as American citizens, they do have the right to vote, work, and go to school without special papers saying they can be in the country. Nia's mom can use her voting power to advocate for immigrant rights so that Yuri and Heejung's families can safely chase their dreams. This is what it means to use one's relative privilege (access to advantages) to make room for all. Every person has privileges that they can use to help make life easier, happier, or safer for others. **Think back to the parts of who you are that make you, you. Which of those identities come with privilege? How can you use your privileges to be an ally to a friend?**

Let's Learn Together!
Page-By-Page Book Discussion Guide

People have different abilities that affect the way they move, see, hear, speak, and learn new things. For example, Allie uses a wheelchair to move about her daily life. Her friends make sure that activities are **accessible** and **available** to people with different abilities and needs so that everyone who wants to join in, can!

On page 16, we see two kinds of work that parents do to make sure children are safe and happy: Allie's mom is cooking, which is care work inside the home, and Parker's mom is creating a computer program for her boss, which is work-for-hire outside the home. Care work and working outside of the home are two ways that parents show their love. **Community care** or **collective parenting** is when families share care work, like Allie and Parker's moms do on this page. Community care helps Parker's mom manage all the things she has to do at her office and at home after work.

Communities are made up of your friends, family, neighbors, classmates, teammates, and anyone else you spend time with. When you're a member of a community, you should do your part to make your community stronger, safer, and more inclusive. When a community is **inclusive**, it makes everyone feel welcome, no matter their skin color, ability, culture, gender, or citizenship. **Think about the people you see and spend time with. Who is part of your community? How do they make you feel stronger, safer, and included? What are some ways you can help make your community better for everyone who is a part of it?**

Book Notes Continued

Sex and gender are related, but they are not the same. A person's **sex** refers to having male, female, or intersex (both male and female) body parts.

Gender is something people show or do through their clothing, behavior, and what they call themselves. When we are born, our gender is often decided for us based on our sex, and sometimes, this affects what we wear or even the toys we play with. You may be familiar with two major gender categories: masculine and feminine. But at any point in our lives, we can choose to identify with one gender, multiple genders, or neither gender. Some people choose to change genders, which is called being **transgender**. And sometimes, when you feel both masculine and feminine, like Kate in this book, it's called being **non-binary**. Non-binary means not being limited to the two categories of masculinity and femininity.

A person can decide to use gendered pronouns like he/his/him and she/hers/her to describe themselves, or they can use non-binary pronouns like they/their/them or ze/zir/zirs. Kate prefers the pronouns they/their/them. We would respect Kate's choice of pronouns by saying, "Kate's cape makes them feel strong." **What pronouns fit you best?**

A **hijab** is a veil or head covering that some Muslim women and girls wear in public. Hijabs come in a lot of colors and styles. Women wear hijabs for many different reasons, like tradition, fashion, or modesty. Professor Saba Mahmood has written about the multiple meanings behind wearing a hijab within the Egyptian Muslim women's movement, and how it can stand for both female empowerment and respect for religious beliefs.

Every culture and community gives meanings to dress and style. One way to gain respect for different groups of people across the world is to think about why their clothing is important to them and their cultures. **What are some of the things people wear in your culture or community that have a special meaning? Ask an adult if you aren't sure and want to learn more.**

People deserve to be safe, no matter what they wear. Through social movements like #MeToo and Times Up, many women (and some others too!) are using their experiences to explain the importance of having **consent**, or permission, before touching another person.

Pages 22 to 25 feature prominent grassroots social movements. **Social movements** are when groups get together to change an unjust or unfair situation. Social movements are made possible by **activists** like Nia and Dakota, who are willing to take a stand for what they believe in. Anyone can be an activist and support a social movement, even you! **Ask an adult to help you learn about some of the issues people in your own community have fought for in the past, like civil rights, environmental sustainability, peace, and marriage equality. What is a cause you believe is worth fighting for? What are some ways that you can take a stand?**

Nia is participating in the **#BlackLivesMatter** movement, which was started by Alicia Garza, Patrisse Cullors, and Opal Tometi in 2013 to bring attention to the violence and racism that Black people face in the United States. This is not just a race issue; it's a gender one too. In fact, Kimberlé Crenshaw first made up the word **intersectionality** to describe how the criminal justice system treats Black women and girls like Nia and her mom differently than Black men and white women. That's why Dr. Crenshaw co-founded the African American Policy Forum (AAPF), a group that is working hard to make sure we protect and empower girls of color through initiatives like #SayHerName.

Dakota is participating in the **Dakota Access Pipeline protests**, also known as **#NoDAPL**, which began in 2016 to stop the construction of an oil pipeline that threatened the Standing Rock Lakota Sioux tribe's ancient burial grounds and water source. As community members, we have the right to disagree with anyone's decisions, even government decisions. Concerned groups make their opinions heard and known by contacting politicians, creating signs, chanting in unison, or simply standing together. The water protectors of #NoDAPL did just that, and the movement became the largest intertribal Native American gathering in modern history! **Are there any rules you think are unfair, or that do not represent the needs of your community? Can you think of ways to make the rule more fair for everybody? Figure out the person or group of people who is responsible for making the rule, and write them a letter explaining what you think should change and why. (Bonus activity: Find allies who agree with you and ask them if they will support your letter by signing their name next to yours.)**

Solidarity is when people with different identities and abilities come together to work towards the same goal. During the 2016 Dakota Access Pipeline (#NoDAPL) protests, another community was protesting their unclean water supply not too far away in the city of Flint, Michigan. In this book, we see Dakota and Nia come together as **allies** to fight for a need they both share—the right to drink clean water. We're always stronger together! **Think about a time when a friend stood up for you when you needed help. What did they do to support you? How did their act of solidarity make you feel? What are some ways you can be an ally in return by supporting them too? (Hint: It helps to ask them what they need first!)**

Pages 30 to 37 all focus on experiences of **migration**, or movement from one place to another. The "**1.5 generation**" describes people who move to a new country when they're children. They are in between the **first generation**, who emigrate as adults, and the second generation, who are born in a new country and have immigrant parents. In this book, Gloria is a second-generation immigrant, while Heejung and Yuri are both part of the 1.5 generation. **Ask your family members about your family's history. Were your parents, grandparents, or ancestors born in the same place as you? How and why did your family end up living where they do now?**

Book Notes Continued

Gloria's story features **generational resources**, which are special skills kids can use to help people who are older than them. Gloria's story is based on what Professor Emir Estrada learned when she talked to immigrant children who sell food and other things with their parents. She found out that these children use their savvy with technology like cell phones and computers to make work easier for their parents. When Gloria uses a smartphone in this book, it shows her generational resources in action.

Like many 1.5 generation immigrants, Heejung is **bilingual**. This means she can speak two languages. When Heejung translates conversations from English to Korean for her mother, she is being a **language broker**. Professor Hyeyoung Kwon talked to many language brokers for her research. She learned that translating for adults is a big responsibility for a kid, because it means knowing more about grown-up responsibilities like paying rent and healthcare than most other children do. Like Gloria and Heejung, we can show people that we care about them by helping them get through difficult situations. **Everybody has skills that can be used to help others. Think about a special talent or ability that you have. How can you use that skill to assist your parents, grandparents, or guardians?**

A **refugee** is a person who has had to leave their home country to be safe from violence, discrimination, or natural disaster. While this book was being written, millions of refugees from the Middle East, North Africa, and Central America were forced to leave their home countries. When so many refugees are forced to leave at the same time like that, families from different countries can help out by volunteering to host people like Yuri and her family in their homes, donating goods, or giving funds to organizations that help refugees. **Find out which organizations help people in need in your area. Can you volunteer your time or donate supplies to support one of these groups? If so, see if you can get some friends to join you!**

A **norm** is a situation that is usual or typical. Even though it can be easy to take what what you see every day for granted, what people think is normal may not always be what is best for everyone, or even most people. When norms are unfair or hurtful, we should do our best to help our communities make a positive change.

What Is a Feminist?

A feminist is a person who believes in equality for people of all genders, and that every person should be able to decide what's best for their own life and future.

What's in a Name?

Adilah is an Arabic name, meaning "justice." The name **Dakota** means "friend" or "ally," and it derives from the Lakota Sioux language. The name **Nia** means "purpose," and it comes from Swahili, which is a language spoken in Kenya. **Where does your name come from? What does your name say about you? If you could change your name, what would you change it to and why?**

Chelsea Johnson

As a kid, I was often the only Black girl in my classrooms. Growing up as an "outsider within" my mostly white schools piqued my interest in how race, class, and gender shape social life. I gained the tools to understand my experiences as an undergraduate at Spelman College, a Historically Black College for women in Atlanta, Georgia. It was at Spelman that I became a feminist. After graduating, I began a PhD in sociology at the University of Southern California. My dissertation explored how fashion, politics, and culture relate. I traveled around the world, interviewing women with African roots in South Africa, Brazil, the Netherlands, France, Spain, and the United States about their lives. I now use research to help companies design products with underrepresented groups in mind. When I'm not researching or writing, I enjoy watercolor painting, reading fiction, and eating my way through new cities.

LaToya Council

I was raised in a single-parent, mother-headed home. I would often stare at my mother in awe of her super-shero abilities to manage so many family demands while holding multiple jobs to make ends meet. These memories inspired my vision for a more inclusive world and drove me toward studying sociology at Spelman College, where I first learned about the concept of intersectionality. After graduating from Spelman, I studied the inequalities in love and how race, gender, and class intersect to inform relationship experiences for my master's at the University of Colorado - Colorado Springs. I am currently working on my dissertation at the University of Southern California, which examines time use and self-care among Black middle-class couples. Intersectionality and the power of love frame how I do allyship and research. When not researching, I enjoy practicing meditation, cooking, and hanging with my cat Mimi.

Carolyn Choi

The Los Angeles Riots were a defining moment in my childhood that shaped my identity as a second generation Korean American woman. My personal experiences with race, immigration, and gender led to me to study sociology and Korean literature at UCLA. After graduating from college, I began community-based organizing at a local non-profit civil rights organization in Los Angeles, which served as my first exposure to intersectional issues facing women in the immigrant community. After earning a master's degree from the London School of Economics and Political Science, I entered doctoral study in sociology at the University of Southern California, where I study the issues of migrant labor, human trafficking, and international education. My research has taken me across the United States, South Korea, the Philippines, and Australia. In my spare time, I enjoy spreading greater awareness about the Korean arts through performing pansori, a form of traditional folk music.

Ashley Seil Smith

I grew up one of five girls (and a twin!) in Southern California and Texas. My conservative roots prompted questions about privilege and feminism, which led me to study cultural anthropology as an undergraduate, including ethnographic research on women's health in South India. I eventually moved to New York City and helped launch The Period Store as a vehicle to educate women about all of their options for period management, while also earning my MFA from the School of Visual Arts. I now focus solely on art, exploring both figuration (drawings that represent things in the real world) and abstraction (drawings from imagination that don't look exactly like things from the real world) to express ideas and tell stories. I embrace all artistic tools and frequently use a variety of media. When I'm not drawing, painting, or print making, you can find me outside being active or caring for my menagerie of adopted senior animals with the help of my husband, Nate.

INSPIRED BY...

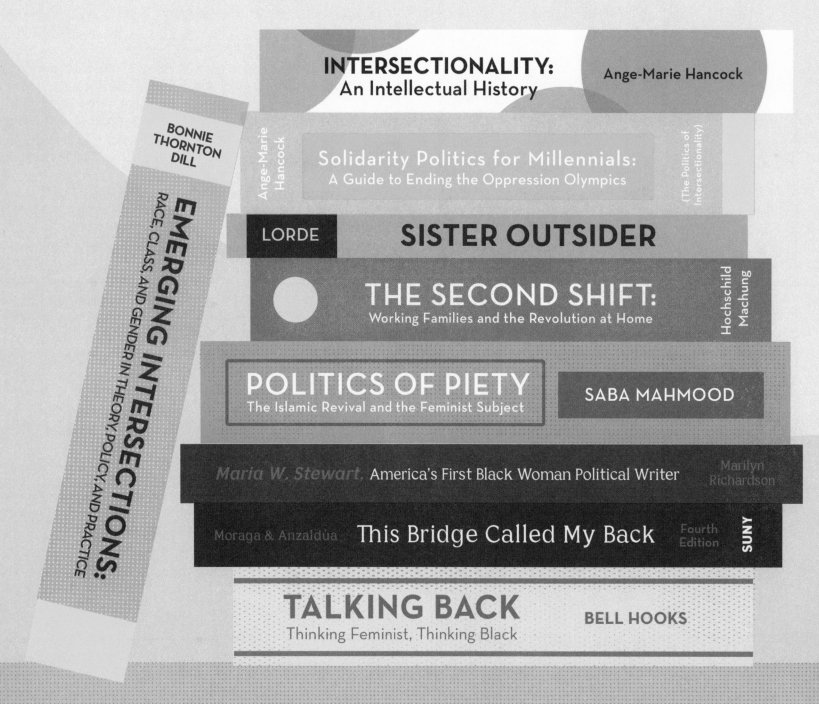

EMERGING INTERSECTIONS:
RACE, CLASS, AND GENDER IN THEORY, POLICY, AND PRACTICE

BONNIE THORNTON DILL

INTERSECTIONALITY:
An Intellectual History

Ange-Marie Hancock

Ange-Marie Hancock

(The Politics of Intersectionality)

Solidarity Politics for Millennials:
A Guide to Ending the Oppression Olympics

LORDE — SISTER OUTSIDER

THE SECOND SHIFT:
Working Families and the Revolution at Home

Hochschild Machung

POLITICS OF PIETY
The Islamic Revival and the Feminist Subject

SABA MAHMOOD

Maria W. Stewart, America's First Black Woman Political Writer

Marilyn Richardson

Moraga & Anzaldúa — This Bridge Called My Back — Fourth Edition — SUNY

TALKING BACK
Thinking Feminist, Thinking Black

BELL HOOKS

UNLEARNING ORIENTALISM   Kathleen Uno

A BURST OF LIGHT   and Other Essays   AUDRE LORDE

Kimberlé Crenshaw

ON INTERSECTIONALITY – *ESSENTIAL WRITINGS* –

FEMINISM WITHOUT BORDERS   Decolonizing Theory, Practicing Solidarity   CHANDRA TALPADE MOHANTY

by bell hooks   **AIN'T I A WOMAN**   black women and feminism

INCIDENTS IN THE LIFE OF A SLAVE GIRL   HARRIET JACOBS

ANGELA Y. DAVIS   **FREEDOM IS A CONSTANT STRUGGLE**

PATRICIA HILL COLLINS   **BLACK FEMINIST THOUGHT**   R

Melissa V. Harris-Perry   Sister Citizen

Acknowledgments

Thank you to all of the feminists who inspired this book, especially our colleagues and mentors at the University of Southern California. These scholars have made room for us.

Thank you to Dr. Kimberlé Crenshaw, who has dedicated her career to "making room" within communities and conversations and whose example of scholar-activism ignited us to move past theory and towards impact. Thank you to Dr. Ange-Marie Hancock Alfaro for your immediate and unwavering belief in us. You blazed the trail we are treading now, and you've looked back to light our way. We hope this book motivates the next generation of intersectional feminists to fight for representation, inclusion, and social justice the way that Dr. Crenshaw and Dr. Hancock Alfaro inspired us.

This book would not have been possible if it were not for our family, friends, and communities, who supported us endlessly. They have truly demonstrated a habit of solidarity by reading and commenting on multiple drafts, attending our community readings, and donating their energy and love. A special thanks to Jonathan Rabb, John Jaeyong Choi, Sasānēhsaeh Pyawasay, Hyeyoung Kwon, Emir Estrada, Kit Myers, Brandy Jenner, Robert Chlala, Dario Valles, Soo Mee Kim, DaniRae Jones, Angel Chang, and Zuri Adele for your help and support during the early stages of *IntersectionAllies* to ensure that each character rang true. Your time and dedication made this project a genuine example of intersectionality and allyship.

We can't thank you all enough.